This book belongs to:

Ellie
....

Stars

and other stories

Ladybird Books

Published by the Penguin Group: London, New York, Australia,
Canada, India, Ireland, New Zealand and South Africa
Penguin Books Ltd, Registered Offices: 80 Strand, London WC2R ORL, England

ladybird.com

First published 2014
ISBN 978-0-72329-842-7
002

This book is based on the
TV series *Peppa Pig*
Peppa Pig is created by
Neville Astley and Mark Baker

Peppa Pig © Astley Baker Davies Ltd/
Entertainment One UK Ltd 2003

www.peppapig.com

Contents

Stars

It is almost time for bed. Mummy Pig, Daddy
Pig and Peppa are having mugs of
hot milk. "Snort! Snort!" George comes
running in wearing his spacesuit!

"George! Why are you in that spacesuit?"
asks Daddy. "You should be in your pyjamas!"
"Hee! Hee! Snort! Snort!"
George loves everything to do with space.

Clunk! Clunk! Oh dear! George is
trying to drink through his helmet.
"George!" cries Peppa. "Take your space
helmet off to drink your milk."

Peppa takes George's helmet off. Slurp!
Slurp! Burp! That's better!
"It's bedtime, little ones!" calls Daddy Pig.

9

Peppa and George are tucked up in bed.
George likes to listen to his space mobile.
"Not space again!" sighs Peppa. "It's boring!"
"Space isn't boring, Peppa. It's full of
wonderful stars!" smiles Daddy Pig.

"Snort! I can't see anything," says Peppa,
looking out of the bedroom window.
"It's easier to see the stars outside,"
explains Daddy Pig. "If you put your
coats on, we could go and see."

"That one is the North Star," says Daddy Pig.
Peppa sings a star song, "North Star!
North Star! Are you near, or are you far?
Can we get there in the car?"
"The stars are too far to get to by car, but they
look closer through a telescope," replies Daddy.

"Grandpa Pig has a telescope," says Mummy Pig.
"It's late, but we can drive to his house, just this once."
"Look!" says Daddy. "We're following the North Star."
"North Star! North Star! Shining with a
twinkly glow. Please show us the way to go."

Peppa and George have arrived at
Granny and Grandpa Pig's house.
Mummy Pig rings the doorbell. Ding! Dong!
"What are you doing here?" asks Grandpa.

"Could we take a look through your
telescope, please?" asks Mummy Pig.
"Very well," replies Grandpa.
"To the top of the house we go!"

Grandpa Pig's hobby is looking at the stars.
"Snort! Here she is! Old Bess!" says Grandpa Pig.
"Wow!" gasps Peppa, seeing the telescope.
"Who's for the first look?" asks Grandpa.
"Me, me, me!" shouts Peppa.

"It's the North Star!" cries Peppa. "We sailors use that star to find our way home," explains Grandpa Pig. "Daddy used it to find his way here," Peppa adds, smiling.

Now, it is George's turn to look through
the telescope. He can see a planet with rings.

"Snort! What else is in the sky?" asks Peppa.
"George can see the planet Saturn," says Grandpa.
"What is Saturn like?" cries Peppa.

"Saturn has rings made of rock and ice and it is very, very cold!" says Grandpa Pig. "We could build a snowman!" cries Peppa. "Quick! Look, Peppa!" gasps Grandpa. "It's a shooting star. You have to make a wish . . ."

"I wish that when George is old enough to have his own rocket, he will take me into space!" cheers Peppa, happily.
"Snort! Snort!" grunts George.
"Ha ha! Snort!" Everyone laughs!

Nature Trail

Peppa and her family are going on a
nature trail. Mummy Pig asks
Daddy Pig not to forget the picnic.
"As if I would," laughs Daddy Pig.

They head off along the trail with their map.
Oh dear! Daddy Pig has left the picnic in the car.

Mummy and Daddy Pig ask Peppa if she can
see anything interesting in the forest.
"I don't see anything but boring trees," says Peppa.
Then she looks really hard and
finds some footprints on the ground.

"Let's follow the footprints and see who
made them," says Mummy Pig.

"We will have to be very quiet so we don't
scare anything away. Shhhh!"

35

Peppa and George follow the footprints along the ground. "It looks like they were made by a little bird," says Mummy Pig.

Soon, they come to the end of the footprints. "The bird has flown up into that tree," smiles Daddy Pig.

"Where?" asks Peppa. Daddy Pig gives Peppa binoculars to help her see the bird.

George finds some more footprints.
They are very little. Daddy Pig says they
belong to ants collecting leaves to eat.

"I think it's time for lunch," says Mummy Pig. But Daddy Pig has left the picnic in the car!

"My map is wrong," begins Daddy Pig. "We'll have to follow our own footprints back to the car."

Suddenly, it starts to rain.
Everyone's footprints are washed away!
"How are we going to find the car, now?"
asks Mummy Pig.

Quack!

Quack!

"Ducks love picnics," says Peppa. "Mrs Duck, can you help us find our picnic please?"

The ducks lead Peppa and her
family back to their car.

"We're here! Thank you for your
help Mrs Duck," cries Peppa.

49

"I love picnics!" laughs Daddy Pig.
The ducks love picnics too.
Quack! Quack! So do the birds!

And so do the ants!

Munch! Munch!

"Everybody loves picnics!" cries Peppa.

Daddy Pig's Old Chair

The school roof has a hole in it. "We are going to have a jumble sale," announces Madame Gazelle.

"The money we raise will pay for a new roof."
Everybody has to bring something to sell.

Later, Peppa is in her bedroom choosing a toy to give
to the jumble sale. "Mr Dinosaur!" she decides.

Everybody gasps and George bursts into tears.
"You can't give away Mr Dinosaur," says Mummy Pig.

"Why don't you give your old jack-in-the-box?" suggests Daddy Pig.

"Oh. OK," agrees Peppa. "Now it's your turn Daddy. What are you going to give?"

Daddy Pig is not sure.
"What about your old squeaky chair?"
suggests Peppa helpfully.

"But it's very old and valuable," says Daddy Pig.
"Hee hee," says Mummy Pig. "You found it
on a rubbish tip!"

When Madame Gazelle arrives in her truck, Mummy Pig, Peppa and George give her everything to take to the jumble sale.

Naughty Mummy Pig gives her Daddy's
squeaky chair too. "Daddy Pig will never notice,"
she whispers to Peppa.

It is the day of the jumble sale.
There are lots of things to buy.

Mummy Pig wants to buy some fruit and vegetables.
Daddy Pig wants to buy a chocolate cake.

"Peppa," says Miss Rabbit.
"How about buying this chair?
It's a bit of rubbish but you can chop
it up and use it for firewood."

"But Daddy says it's very old and worth lots of money!" says Peppa.

All Peppa's friends have given something to the jumble sale. Suzy has given her nurse's outfit.

Pedro has given his balloon
and Candy has given her aeroplane.

"I will miss my jack-in-the-box," sighs Peppa.
"I will miss playing at nurses," says Suzy sadly.

Peppa's friends all think they will miss
their toys, so they buy them back again.

"Look what I've bought!" snorts Daddy Pig.
"It's an antique chair to match my old one!"

"Oh, Daddy Pig!" laughs Mummy Pig.
"It matches your old one because it
IS your old one!" snorts Peppa.

"But Miss Rabbit has just charged me lots of money for it!" says poor Daddy Pig. "Fantastic news!" says Madame Gazelle.

"We have just raised all the money
we need for a new school roof!"
"Hooray!" everybody cheers.

Recycling Fun

Mr Bull, the binman, is collecting
the rubbish. It's early in the morning
so he tries to be as quiet as he can.

79

Crash, clank!

But Mr Bull is not very good at being quiet.
"Hello, Mr Bull," snort Daddy Pig,
Peppa and George.

"Hello, everyone," says Mr Bull.

Peppa and George are helping to
clear up the breakfast things.
"We don't put bottles in the rubbish bin.
They can be recycled," says Mummy Pig.

Soon they have collected
enough things, so Peppa and
her family set off for the
recycling centre.

Mummy Pig has the bottles and
Peppa has the tin cans.
George has the newspapers.

"Is everybody ready?" asks Daddy Pig.
"Yes!" shout Peppa and George.

Clink, clink, rattle, rattle, rustle, rustle!

Soon, they arrive at Miss Rabbit's recycling centre.
Miss Rabbit is sitting high up inside a big crane.
She is busy recycling all the rusty old cars.
It is very noisy.

"Who knows which bin the bottles
go in?" asks Mummy Pig.

"And the cans go in the blue one!" says Peppa. "Well done, Peppa," smiles Mummy Pig.

Rattle! Rattle!

"Where's our car gone?" asks Daddy Pig.
"Stand back!" shouts Miss Rabbit from up
above them. Miss Rabbit is about
to recycle Peppa's car!

"Stop!"
shouts Peppa.
"Our car isn't old
and rusty!"

"Ha! Ha! Silly me!" says Miss Rabbit.
"I just love recycling."
"So do we!" laughs Peppa.
"But we also love our little car!"

School Bus Trip

Peppa and her friends are
going on a school bus trip.

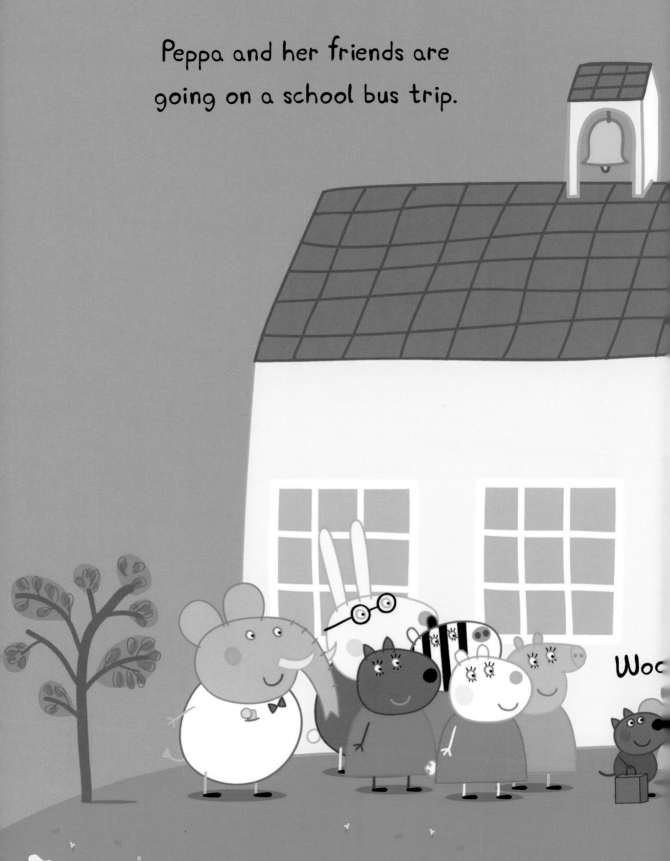

Woo

"Let's check you are all here,"
says Madame Gazelle.
"Here!" cries Peppa.

Baaa! Grunt! Snort!

"Today," begins Madame Gazelle,
"we are going on a trip to the mountains!"

"Hooray!"

cheer all the children.

Peppa and Suzy are already a little hungry.
"Please can we eat our lunch now?"
they ask Madame Gazelle.

"Why not eat your apples
and save the rest for the picnic?"
she replies. Crunch! Crunch!

The bus has arrived at the foot of
the mountain. The road is very steep!
"Come on bus! You can make it!"
everyone cheers.

Peppa and her friends have finally
made it to the top of the mountain.
"Look at the view!" gasps Madame Gazelle.
All the children look out over the valley.

"Wow!" sighs Peppa, loudly.
"Wow! Wow! Wow!" Peppa hears in the distance.
"What was that?" she asks quietly.
"It's your echo, Peppa!" replies Madame Gazelle.

"An echo is the sound you hear
when you speak loudly in the mountains,"
explains Madame Gazelle.
Grunt! Woof! Baaa! Snort!

Snort!

Grunt! Baaa!

Woof!

Now it's time for a picnic lunch.
Peppa loves picnics.
Everyone loves picnics!
Munch! Slurp! Munch! Yum! Yum!

117

"Where are the ducks?"
asks Peppa, taking a bite of her sandwich.
"They always turn up when we have picnics."

Quack! Quack! Quack!
Here come the ducks.

"Hello! Would you like some bread?"
Peppa asks them. The ducks are very lucky today.
There is plenty of bread!

The bus has arrived.
It's time to go home.

"Let's all sing a song!" suggests
Madame Gazelle. Hooray!
Everyone has had a great day!

Sports Day

Today is school sports day.
Peppa and her friends are all here.

The first event is running.
The children have to run as fast as they can.

"Ready . . . Steady . . . Go!"
says Madame Gazelle.

Suzy and Peppa are chatting about who can run the fastest.

Rebecca Rabbit is in the lead.
Peppa and Suzy are right at the back.

Rebecca Rabbit wins the race!
"Hooray," everyone cheers.
Peppa and Suzy are last.

"It's not the winning that matters,"
Daddy Pig reminds them.
"But the taking part."

"The next event is the long jump,"
says Madame Gazelle.

George and Richard Rabbit have to run
and then jump as far as they can.
Whoever jumps the furthest is the winner.
"Ready . . . Steady . . . Go!"

Oh dear. Richard Rabbit has jumped further than George. "Hooray!" shout all his friends.

George is not happy.
"Remember George," says Peppa.
"It's not the winning that matters
but the taking part."

The next race is the relay.
Daddy Pig is in the lead.
He hands the baton to Peppa.

"Thank you, Daddy, you did very well.
Now it's my turn to . . . " begins Peppa.
"Stop talking and run!" snorts Daddy Pig.

Emily Elephant is the winner!
Everyone cheers. "Hooray!"

Peppa comes last.
She is not feeling happy.

It's the last event of the day, the tug of war.
Boys against girls.
"The girls will win!" snorts Peppa.

"Woof! No they won't!" says Danny.
Everyone is pulling so hard, the rope breaks!

"The result is a draw!
Both teams win!" says Madame Gazelle.
Everybody cheers.

"Hooray!"

"I love school sports day," snorts Peppa,
"Especially when I win a prize!"

Peppa Goes Swimming

It's a lovely sunny day and Peppa and her family are at the swimming pool.

"Peppa! George! Let Daddy put on your armbands," snorts Mummy Pig.

Today is George's first time at the pool and he's a bit scared of getting in.

"Why don't you just put one foot in the water?" suggests Daddy Pig. "Maybe George should try both feet at the same time?" says Mummy Pig.

Splash! Mummy Pig convinces George to jump into the water and he loves it!

"Grunt! Hee! Hee! Snort!"
shouts George, happily.
"Ho! Ho! Well done, George!"
snorts Daddy Pig.

Here is Rebecca Rabbit with her brother, Richard and their mummy.

"Hello, everyone!" cries Rebecca.
"Squeak, squeak," says Richard.

"Richard, hold on to this float
and you can practise kicking your legs,"
says Mummy Rabbit.

"George, would you like to try kicking your legs?" asks Mummy Pig.
"Hee! Hee! Float! Snort!" giggles George.

"Ho! Ho! Very good," laughs Daddy Pig,
"but please try not to splash."
"Grunt! Big children don't splash," adds Peppa.

"Big children are very good at swimming,"
snorts Peppa. "When George and Richard
are older, they'll be able to swim
like us, won't they, Rebecca?"

"Yes!" says Rebecca, as she
watches the boys kicking.

Peppa and Rebecca race each other up
and down the pool with their armbands on.

They are having lots of fun swimming
and splashing in the water.

Oops! Richard has dropped his toy
watering can into the pool.
"Mummy! Wah!" cries Richard.
"Sorry, Richard, I can't reach.
It's too far down," says Mummy Rabbit.
Luckily, Daddy Pig is an excellent swimmer.
He takes off his glasses and dives down to get it.

"Ho! Ho! There you go!"
snorts Daddy Pig.
"Squeak, squeak!" says Richard.

"Well done, Daddy!"
smiles Mummy Pig.

Oh dear! Now Richard is soaking Daddy Pig with the watering can. What a naughty rabbit! "Hee! Hee! Hee!" George thinks it's hilarious. Everyone has had a wonderful day at the pool!

Tiny Creatures

Peppa and George are helping Grandpa Pig pick vegetables. Grandpa hands Peppa a lettuce.

Peppa can see something sitting on the lettuce.
"There's a horrible monster!" she snorts.

"That's just a little snail!" says Grandpa.
"Grrr. Mon-sta!" says George.

George likes the snail.
Suddenly the snail disappears.
"Where's he gone?" asks Peppa.
"He's hiding in his shell," explains Grandpa.

"Grandpa! George and I want
to be snails," says Peppa.

"Well," says Grandpa, "these baskets can be your shells!"
"I'm going to eat up all Grandpa Pig's lettuce!" laughs Peppa.

"Oi! Keep off my lovely lettuce
you cheeky snails!" calls Grandpa.

"And when Grandpa Pig shouts at me," giggles Peppa,
"I'll hide inside my little house!"
"Mon-sta!" says George.

Here are Peppa and
George's friends.
"Can we be snails too?" they ask.

"Well," says Grandpa.
"You could be something
else exciting from the garden."
"What's that buzzing sound?"
asks Peppa.

187

"It's coming from that little house," says Suzy. "It's a bee house," explains Grandpa.

"It's called a hive."

"The bees collect nectar from the flowers and then fly to the hive to make it into honey."

"Hmmmm, I like honey," says Peppa.
"Let's pretend to be bees!
Buzz, buzz, buzz! Ha, ha, ha!"
"What busy bees!" laughs Grandpa.

191

Granny Pig has been baking bread.
"Would you busy bees like some toast?" she asks.

"Yes, please!" say Peppa and her friends.
"With lots of honey!"

"I like being a bee because they eat lots of lovely honey!" says Suzy.

"I like being a snail," snorts Peppa, "because they eat all Grandpa's vegetables!"